★ TWINNING TALES®

DINGLE
&
DANGLE

DINGLE DANGLE means:

swinging backwards and forwards

in a dangling manner…

…hanging loose!

Dingle & Dangle live in New Zealand.

Dingle is a kiwi - round, brown and long-beaked. Dangle is a kakapo - a large greenish parrot with an owl-like face. Dingle gets his name because he lives in a deep wooded valley near Queenstown. Dangle, who lives close by, gets her name because she wears big hoop earrings that *dangle* from her ears. Dingle & Dangle have known each other since nursery school. They like to hang around - not just because they are good friends, but Dingle & Dangle share a common bond - they cannot fly!

"I wish I could fly," dreams Dingle as he looks longingly at the sky. "Me, too, Dingle," imagines Dangle, "me, too!"

Dingle & Dangle are determined to fly. They are fed up watching their friends fly free as birds and soar high above the world. Dingle phones Dangle. "Come over, Dangle," excites Dingle, "I've bought a trampoline to help us fly."

Dingle & Dangle try the trampoline.

"We're flying!" they yell as they jump high into the air. No sooner do they fly than they fall back to earth...with a bump! "Who are we kidding," moans Dingle, "this isn't flying." "Being able to see into the neighbour's garden for a split second...again and again," grumbles Dangle, "isn't what I call flying!"

Dingle & Dangle climb one of the tall trees next to Dingle's house. They perch on a high branch and dangle their feet beneath.

"This is as close to flying as we'll get," remarks Dingle. "Yeah," comments Dangle, "a great view but we must hold on tight in case we fall."

Just as they begin to give up their hope of flying, Dingle & Dangle hear a loud shout. "Geronimo!" screams the shout.

Dingle & Dangle look towards the river. "Someone's flying!" observes Dingle. "Let's go and find out," suggests Dangle as they climb down carefully.

Dingle & Dangle make their way to the river bridge. There is a sign with a picture of someone flying. It reads *Bungee-jumping here. Do you think you can hack it?*

"They're flying," thrills Dingle, "let's give it a go."
The assistant asks, "Do you want to jump together or separately?"
Dingle & Dangle look at each other and smile. "Together!" declares Dangle.

The assistant weighs Dingle & Dangle, attaches long rubbery ropes to their ankles and casually says, "In your own time, Dudes!"

Dingle & Dangle shuffle to the platform edge.

Dingle & Dangle hold each other, and after a count of three, they jump.
"We're flying!" they wail. No sooner do they fly than they fall towards the river.
"We're going to crash into the river!" scares Dingle.
"We're going to drown!" frightens Dangle.
Dingle & Dangle dip into the river and then stop.
The rope recoils and catapults them back towards the bridge.
"We're flying again," Dingle & Dangle cheer, but then they fall again!
They do this several times until they come to a standstill and dingle dangle,
waiting for the assistant to detach them.
"That was fantastic!" fizzes Dangle.
"It was," states Dingle, "but it's not flying!"

Dingle & Dangle make their way back to Dingle's house. They can't stop talking about the bungee-jump.

"I'm going to do that again," decides Dangle.

"Me, too," determines Dingle, "but there must be something closer to flying?"

Just as Dingle finishes his sentence, a fox flies through the air…whizzes over Dingle & Dangles' heads and misses them by a whisker. "Weeeeeee," howls the fox.

"Did you see that, Dangle?" proclaims Dingle, "I've never seen a flying fox!"

"Me, neither," exclaims Dangle. "Only a fox that flies by the seat of his pants!"

Dingle & Dangle watch the fox disappear into the distance. "We've got to give that a go," they enthuse, "it looks more like flying than bungee-jumping."

Dingle & Dangle follow the overhead wire to the top of the hill. There is a sign with a picture of the flying fox. It reads *Zip through the air like you're flying!*

"Like you're flying!" beams Dingle, "Let's do it."

The assistant asks, "Do you want to fly together or separately?" Dingle & Dangle look at each other and smile. "Together!" declares Dangle.

The assistant gives Dingle & Dangle each a helmet, secures them to the harness - Dingle in front of Dangle, and advises, "You'll think you're not going to stop, but I assure you...you will!"

Dingle & Dangle dangle beneath the wire. The assistant gives a push, and off they zip.
"We're flying!" screeches Dingle as they skim the treetops.
"This is amazing," shrieks Dangle as she grips Dingle tightly around the waist.

Dingle & Dangle speed faster and faster over the valley and across the river.
The air blows hard against their faces.
No sooner do they begin to enjoy than they reach the end and stop.
Dingle & Dangle sway from side to side until they come to a complete standstill.

"We've got to do that again," raves Dangle.
"It's great fun," despairs Dingle, "but it's not flying - we just go in a straight line!"

Dingle & Dangle take the cable car to the top of the mountain to have lunch. They cannot stop thinking about the flying fox and their zip-wire ride. They eat a sandwich and look out across the lake.

Suddenly, the view is blocked by a large orange canopy and then by an enormous pink canopy. Dangling beneath each canopy are two possums!

"Look, Dangle," urges Dingle, "those possums are flying!"
"Yes," cries Dangle, "and they're not going in straight lines!"
"We've got to give that a go," they decide, "it looks more like flying than zip-wire riding."

Dingle & Dangle enquire at the information desk.

"We would like to try that, please," pleads Dingle, pointing at the possums.
"Like the paragliding possums?" asks the assistant.
"Yeah, like the pair-of-gliding possums," mishears Dangle.

The assistant gives Dingle & Dangle a leaflet and guides them in the right direction.

Dingle & Dangle find the mountain path and pick up the pace - they cannot wait to fly!

Dingle & Dangle enrol for paragliding.

"Have you done this before?" probes the assistant.

"No," straight-talk Dingle & Dangle.

"It's a load of hot air!" jokes the assistant, "Your canopy catches the rising thermals which makes you fly."

"How do we steer?" dangles Dingle.

"You pull these cords," instructs the assistant. "The left cord turns left, and the right cord turns right."

"Makes sense!" nod Dingle & Dangle.

Finally, the assistant asks, "Do you want to fly together or separately?"

Dingle & Dangle look at each other and smile. "Separately!" declares Dangle.

Dingle takes a running jump and leaps into the air. His blue canopy opens, and he begins to fly. Dangle follows - her red canopy opens, and she starts to fly too.

"We're flying!" delights Dingle as they approach the two possums. "I'm a parrot-gliding!" jests Dangle as she steers left and right.

No sooner do Dingle & Dangle achieve their goal of flying than a squirrel rockets past...wearing a magic suit!

"Did you see that?" Dangle quizzes Dingle, not believing her eyes, "That squirrel's flying!" "We're just dangling from a canopy!" discerns Dingle, "That looks more like flying than paragliding."

Dingle & Dangle make their way to the bottom of the mountain in search of the squirrel.

"Excuse us," Dingle & Dangle approach the squirrel. "We saw you whizz past in some sort of magic suit."

"My wingsuit," replies Ken, the squirrel, "my suit with wings!"

"Where can we get one?" questions Dingle.

"They must be specially made," informs Ken, "to fit like a glove."

"If we get wingsuits," proposes Dangle, "will you show us how to use them?"

"Sure," answers Ken, "I'll show you how to fly!"

Dingle & Dangle look at each other and smile.

Dingle & Dangle and Ken take the cable car to the top of the mountain, climbing further to reach the highest point where the view is full-circle. They put on their wingsuits.

"We must plan our route," surveys Ken. "Have somewhere to aim and to avoid any obstacles!"

"How do we steer?" queries Dingle.

"You've got to *feel* the wind," outlines Ken, "use your left and right wings and your leg wing to make small adjustments."

"Like a real bird," details Dangle, "flexing one way to add *lift* or another to add *drag*."

"Exactly!" praises Ken, "You're going to be naturals!"

"Follow me!" calls Ken as he takes off.

"I'm nervous," worries Dingle.

"We've set our minds on flying," reassures Dangle. "We must be brave and take a leap of faith!"

Dingle & Dangle dive and dart through the sky, moving one way and another - just feet above the ground. Ken leads them through mountain passes, over tree-filled fields and past sheep-eating pastures.

"We're flying!" screams Dingle. "No dangling from ropes or wires or canopies!"

"We sure are!" shouts Dangle. "Using our *wings* to fly wherever we want!"

Dingle & Dangle overflow with joy. They agree to meet Ken the next day to fly again!

Dingle & Dangle make their way back to Dingle's house. "We can fly," Dingle whispers softly, waiting to wake up and find it is all a dream! "Absolutely!" concludes Dangle as she pinches herself to make sure it is true. "Thank goodness we pushed ourselves," applauds Dingle, "and we didn't settle for second best."

"Yes," grins Dangle. "Anything's possible if you put your mind to it."

Dingle & Dangle look at each other and laugh...flying high with excitement.

How uplifting is that!

THE END

NOW LOOK OUT FOR THE NEXT
TWINNING TALE

ROLY & POLY

Printed in Poland
by Amazon Fulfillment
Poland Sp. z o.o., Wrocław

55356744R00016